Dracula

by Bram Stoker

Retold by Dennis Hamley

Illustrated by Kenny McKendry
Series Editors: Steve Barlow and Steve Skidmore

Published by Ginn and Company
Halley Court, Jordan Hill, Oxford OX2 8EJ
A division of Reed Educational and Professional Publishing Ltd

Telephone number for ordering **Impact**: 01865 888084

OXFORD   MELBOURNE   AUCKLAND
JOHANNESBURG   BLANTYRE   GABORONE   IBADAN
PORTSMOUTH (NH) USA   CHICAGO

First published 1999

2003 2002 2001 2000

10 9 8 7 6 5 4 3 2

ISBN 0 435 21229 X

Illustrations
Kenny McKendry/Artist Partners

Cover artwork
Kevin Jenkins

Designed by Shireen Nathoo Design

Printed and bound in Great Britain by
Biddles Ltd, Guildford and King's Lynn

Contents

Characters

Count Dracula is
a strange old man
who lives in a castle
in Transylvania.

Jonathan Harker
is a young
English lawyer.

Mina Murray
is engaged
to Jonathan.

Lucy Westenra
and Mina are
best friends.

Arthur Holmwood is Lucy's boyfriend.

Dr John Seward is a young doctor. He and Arthur are best friends.

Renfield is one of Dr Seward's patients.

Professor Van Helsing used to teach John Seward.

5

CHAPTER 1

Count Dracula's castle

The coachman's eyes were red, and his teeth were long and sharp. He made the horses gallop along narrow mountain roads.

Jonathan Harker held on tight. They went so fast that he thought the coach would crash over the edge. Wolves howled in the forest. The journey seemed endless.

But at last they arrived at Castle Dracula.
It stood high on a jagged mountain top, black
against the moonlight.

Jonathan was a lawyer from Exeter.
Count Dracula had invited him to his castle
in Transylvania. He wanted Jonathan to help
him buy a house in London.

Jonathan entered the castle. At once he felt uneasy. The Count told Jonathan he lived alone. He sat with Jonathan at supper, but did not eat. He watched Jonathan closely. His eyes did not leave him.

Later that evening, they talked about the house in London. It was called Carfax House. It was large and had its own chapel. Jonathan thought the Count looked old and tired. He asked the Count why he wanted to move.

The next morning, something strange happened. Jonathan was shaving when a hand suddenly gripped his shoulder. The Count's voice spoke in his ear. But Jonathan couldn't see him in the mirror!

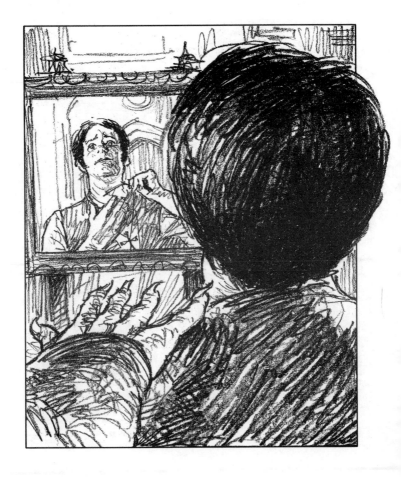

Jonathan cut himself in surprise. The Count saw the blood and grabbed Jonathan's throat.

But then the Count saw a cross around Jonathan's neck. He staggered back. His face was filled with fear. He grabbed the mirror and threw it out of the window.

Jonathan was shocked and confused.

As time went by, more strange things happened. Late one evening he wrote a letter to his fiancée, Mina, back in England.

Castle Dracula
Transylvania
6th May 1897

My dearest Mina

This is the strangest place in the world. Helping people buy houses is usually boring. This time it's frightening.

For in this wild, lonely place, I am afraid. I think I am a prisoner here.

Jonathan looked out of the window and cried out, "Count Dracula, who are you? *What* are you?" He stared down at the drop below. "Will I ever get away?"

Wolves howled outside. Moonlight lit up the castle walls. Then Jonathan saw something climbing out of the Count's window.

Jonathan stared in disbelief.

First came the Count's head. Then came his hands, with long, hooked fingers. Then came his whole body. He was crawling down the wall, face-down! His cloak spread out like the black wings of a bat. He crept like a lizard – down, down, down. Then he disappeared into the black of the night.

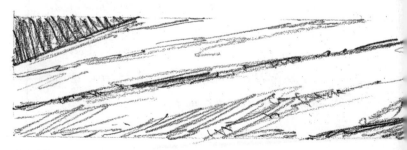

Jonathan went to bed, but he couldn't
sleep. Some time later, he heard a noise in his
room. Three women were standing over him.
They had dark hair, red lips and sharp white
teeth. Their eyes glowed red. Jonathan sat up
in fear.

The women laughed. One of them put her
hand round Jonathan's throat.

Suddenly, the Count appeared. His eyes blazed. "Leave him!" he shouted.

"Is there nothing for us tonight, then?" asked one of the women.

"I haven't forgotten you," said the Count. He threw a sack on the floor. Something in it moved.

Jonathan fainted with terror.

When Jonathan woke the next morning, everything was quiet. He had to find out what was happening!

He climbed out of his window and used cracks in the wall to crawl to the Count's room. He slipped inside and saw some steps. They led down to an old chapel.

Inside the chapel were long wooden boxes. Jonathan lifted two of the lids. The boxes were filled with earth.

But when Jonathan lifted the lid of a third box, he was horrified.

There lay the Count. He looked young again. His hair was dark and shiny. His lips and cheeks were red. He was not breathing. But there were drops of fresh blood on his lips and on those long, white, sharp teeth.

Jonathan slammed the lid shut and rushed out. He climbed back to his room, feeling sick with terror. He knew he must escape back to England. But the castle was surrounded by high mountains, and there were wolves in the forest. It would not be easy.

CHAPTER 2

Death is in the air

In Exeter, Mina Murray was worried. Jonathan's letter from Castle Dracula made her feel uneasy.

But she also had good news from Lucy Westenra, her friend who lived in London.

Dearest Mina
I'm so thrilled. Today Arthur has asked me to marry him...

Mina was pleased for her friend. She wrote back to Lucy at once.

Dearest Lucy

I am so happy for you. But I'm also worried. Jonathan has not come back. His letters are strange and not like him at all. Something terrible has happened. I know it.

When Lucy read Mina's letter, she wanted to be with her. "Mother," she said. "Can Mina come on holiday with us to Whitby? It might cheer her up. I wish Arthur could come, too. But his father is too ill."

"Of course she can come," said Lucy's mother.

A month later, Lucy and Mina were together in North Yorkshire, by the sea.

One evening in Whitby, dark clouds gathered over the sea. A storm was brewing.

"Death is in the air," the local fishermen said.

That night Mina hardly slept. She was still worried about Jonathan. The rain and thunder kept her awake. Lightning flashed and huge waves beat against the harbour walls.

The next day, Mina read a strange newspaper report.

8TH AUGUST 1897

MYSTERY SHIP WRECKED

A cargo ship was wrecked in last night's storm. Only the captain was found on board. His dead body was tied to the ship's wheel. Onlookers say they saw a huge beast run away from the ship.

"It was like a wolf," said an eyewitness. "I was scared stiff." The creature has not been seen since.

The ship's log tells of a trip of terror. Crew members thought a ghost was on board. All the sailors went missing one by one until only the captain was left.

Fifty boxes like coffins were found on the ship. They were addressed to a house in London and will be sent on by train.

Mina remembered what the locals had
said the day before – 'Death is in the air.'
Suddenly, she was afraid.

That night, Mina slept badly again. She suddenly woke up as the clock struck midnight. Something was wrong.

Mina and Lucy shared a room and Lucy's bed was empty. Mina leaped out of bed and ran to the window. She saw Lucy on a path that led to the East Cliff.

Mina pulled on a shawl and followed her. Before long, she saw Lucy sitting on a stone bench. Something was leaning over her.

At first, Mina thought it might be a
shadow or a trick of the light. But it wasn't.

In the moonlight, Mina could make out a
white face and red eyes. It scared her even to
look at it.

Then the moon disappeared behind a
cloud. When the cloud had passed, the
strange figure had gone.

Mina wrapped her shawl around Lucy
and guided her home. Lucy seemed to be
asleep. But she kept touching her throat.

When Lucy woke up late the next
morning, Mina asked her what had happened.
Lucy couldn't remember anything about it.

But Mina saw that Lucy had two tiny
holes in her neck. As she looked at them,
her fear returned.

After that, Mina slept badly every night. She heard a strange scratching at the window as if something was trying to get in. One night she saw a huge bat at the window.

Mina grew more and more worried about Lucy. Since her midnight walk, Lucy had been quiet and very pale. Mina decided to write to Arthur. She told him about Lucy's illness and the other strange things that were happening.

A week later, a letter arrived for Mina about Jonathan.

"Jonathan's safe!" she cried to Lucy. "He's being treated at a hospital in Budapest." Then her voice dropped. "But they say he needs rest. He has been through bad times. I wonder what happened? It doesn't say."

Then Mina's face lit up. "I'll go to Budapest. We can be married there and then I'll bring him home!"

But Lucy was still pale and weak and could hardly smile. Everyone was worried about her.

"We must go home to London," Lucy's mother said. "Lucy needs a doctor. Perhaps Arthur's friend, Dr Seward, will know what the matter is."

So the holiday came to an end. Lucy and her mother left for London. Mina got ready for her journey to Budapest.

CHAPTER 3

Tooth-marks

Back in London, Dr John Seward was working in a hospital for the insane. It was next door to Carfax House – the house that Count Dracula had bought.

Dr Seward went to see Lucy as soon as he heard about her illness. He was puzzled. "I don't understand Lucy's illness," he said. "She can't rise from her bed. She's pale and weak, as if there's no blood in her veins. I'll send for my old teacher from Amsterdam, Professor Van Helsing. He'll know what is wrong."

Three days later, the Professor arrived. Dr Seward showed him the marks on Lucy's neck.

The Professor told Dr Seward not to leave Lucy on her own. "I fear great harm might come to her," he said.

Dr Seward watched Lucy all night. Nothing happened. As he watched, he wrote in his notebook.

Now I have two patients I can't understand. One is Lucy. The other is a man at the hospital called Renfield. He is acting strangely. First he ate nothing but flies. Now he has started to eat spiders.

Before I left the hospital last night, he was staring through his bars. "The Master is near," he cried. What did he mean?

Thank goodness Lucy seems a little better this morning.

Lucy seemed much better by the end of the day.

"I don't need to watch her tonight," Dr Seward told Lucy's mother. "I shall sleep in the next room."

But next morning, the Professor arrived early and woke him up. "Come quickly," the Professor said. "Something terrible has happened."

Lucy was deathly pale. Her lips stretched back over her teeth. The marks on her neck were red. The Professor felt her pulse.

She's only just alive!

When Lucy woke, the Professor gave her some flowers. Lucy smelled them. "These are garlic," she said.

"Garlic can protect you," the Professor replied. "Our enemy hates and fears it." He spread more garlic around the room and smeared it on the window frames. He turned to Dr Seward. "She will be safe tonight."

Later that evening, Arthur arrived. The
Professor and Dr Seward took him to see
Lucy. Before they could enter the room, Lucy's
mother appeared.

"Why did you leave those smelly plants in
Lucy's room?" she asked. "I took them away
and opened the windows to let in some fresh
air."

The three men rushed in. Lucy was hardly
breathing.

The Professor told Lucy's mother that the garlic was to protect Lucy. It should stay in her room at all times. After that, a week passed and nothing strange happened.

But Dr Seward was very worried about Renfield, his strange patient at the hospital. He was getting worse. Renfield attacked Dr Seward with a knife, then tried to lick up the blood.

Soon after, a telegram came for
Dr Seward. It was from the Professor. It told
Dr Seward to watch over Lucy that night. But
the telegram arrived a day late. The night had
passed without Dr Seward being there!

Dr Seward hurried to Lucy's house and
rushed into her room. An awful sight met his
eyes. Two bodies lay on the bed. One was
Lucy's mother. She was dead. The other was
Lucy. She was dying.

Lucy clutched a letter in her hand.
Dr Seward took it. As he read it, his blood
ran cold.

*I write while I can. I was woken by a bat.
Its wings were beating on the window.*

*Mother came into my room. "I heard
a noise," she said. "I'll keep you company."*

*Suddenly, a huge wolf's head
crashed through the window. Mother
screamed. In her fear, she knocked away
the garlic I was wearing to protect me.*

*Then a whirling mist came towards
me. Two red eyes stared out of it. Mother
fell across me and I knew no more.*

*Now I am awake again. Mother lies
here dead. I know that once I close my eyes,
I shall never open them again. Goodbye, my
dear Arthur...*

Lucy lay unconscious for two days.
Arthur, Dr Seward and the Professor took it
in turns to watch over her.

On the evening of the second day, the Professor called them to her bedside. The toothmarks on her neck had disappeared.

The next morning, Lucy's lips had stretched back. They saw that her teeth were long, sharp and white. She took one last breath. Then she died.

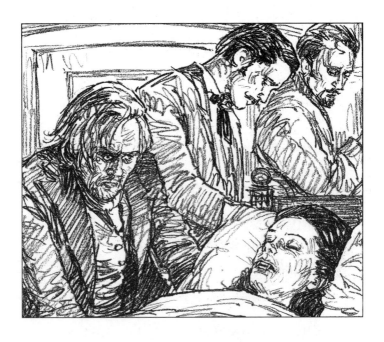

Lucy and her mother were laid to rest together in the family vault.

The terror spreads

Two months had passed since Mina left for Budapest. She and Jonathan had got married and were on their way back home.

Mina was looking forward to seeing Lucy again. She had no idea that Lucy was dead. Jonathan was feeling better, but was often tired. He had not yet told Mina what had happened at Count Dracula's castle.

They travelled through London on their way to Devon. As they got into a cab to go to the station, Jonathan suddenly gripped Mina's arm. He pointed at a tall man with a dark beard, red lips and very sharp teeth.

"It's the Count I met at the castle," Jonathan gasped. "But he's young again!"

When they arrived home, a letter was waiting for Jonathan and Mina. It was from the Professor. He told them that Lucy and her mother were dead, and asked to see Mina urgently.

Mina wept for her dead friend. That night, she couldn't sleep. She found Jonathan's diary and began to read about his trip to Castle Dracula. Soon she wondered if she would ever sleep again.

The Professor arrived the next day and told them more about Lucy. Mina told him about Jonathan's diary and he asked to read it. He read all night.

In the morning, he told Mina, "All your husband writes is true."

"Do you think the Count has something to do with Lucy's death?"

"I fear so," replied the Professor.

Later that day, Mina and Jonathan took the Professor to catch a train back to London.

At the station, the Professor bought a newspaper. He looked at the front page. His face turned pale with horror.

"Oh, no, not so soon!" he cried.

8TH AUGUST 1897

MYSTERY ON HAMPSTEAD HEATH

Another child playing on Hampstead Heath disappeared yesterday evening. He was found again in the morning. Parents are being warned to keep their children indoors.

The child was unharmed except for two slight wounds in the neck.

These wounds look like small bites from a rat or dog.

The child has no memory of what happened. He only said that a "beautiful lady" had taken him for a walk.

The police have not found out who this lady is.

When the Professor arrived in London, he went to see Dr Seward. He showed him the newspaper report. "Do the marks on the boy's neck remind you of anything?" he asked.

"They remind me of the marks on Lucy's neck," said Dr Seward. "But surely this has nothing to do with Lucy's death?"

"I'm afraid it has," answered the Professor. "Lucy made those marks."

Dr Seward was shocked. "That's impossible!" he cried.

"I can prove it. Follow me!" the Professor said.

The Professor took Dr Seward to the vault where Lucy's body was laid. He unlocked the door. The Professor unscrewed the lid of Lucy's coffin. It was empty! Dr Seward gasped. "Who could have done this?" he asked. "Body snatchers?"

"No, it is much worse," the Professor replied. "You will see."

They replaced the coffin lid and waited outside. Hours passed until midnight came. Suddenly, a white shape glided towards the tomb. It carried a bundle.

The Professor turned to Dr Seward. "Stay here!" he said. Then he disappeared into the night.

Dr Seward heard a terrible shriek in the darkness. He felt a chill run up his spine.

A few moments later the Professor returned. He was trembling and pale. He carried a small child in his arms.

We were just in time! There are no marks on his throat. We must leave this dreadful place. Tomorrow, we shall return.

The next afternoon, they returned to Lucy's coffin. The Professor again lifted off the coffin lid. This time, Lucy lay inside. She looked as beautiful as if she were alive. Her lips were red, and her teeth were white and as sharp as a dog's.

"Do you see?" the Professor asked Dr Seward. "She is un-dead. She was bitten by a vampire. Now she is a vampire herself, living off the blood of others."

"What can we do?" asked Dr Seward.

"We must drive a wooden stake through her heart," the Professor replied. "Then we must cut off her head. Finally, we must fill her mouth with garlic."

Dr Seward shuddered. "Then let us do it," he said.

Arthur arrived the next day. The Professor repeated what he had told Dr Seward. Arthur felt angry, but at last he agreed to go with them.

Just before midnight, the Professor, Dr Seward and Arthur were waiting outside the vault. At the stroke of twelve, a silent figure appeared.

"Lucy!" Arthur gasped.

"No!" The Professor gripped his arm. "What you see is no longer Lucy. Watch!"

The white figure seemed to melt through the closed door of the vault. They waited. Then they opened the door and went to Lucy's coffin. The Professor unscrewed the lid. There she lay. Even Arthur hated what he saw. "Now I understand," he cried. "I know what I must do."

Arthur held the sharp stake high above Lucy's heart. Then, with all his strength, he hammered it down. The thing in the coffin screamed horribly, but was soon still.

The Professor cut off the head and stuffed the mouth with garlic. "Now we must find and destroy Dracula."

CHAPTER 5

The vampire must die!

Mina and Jonathan came to London and joined the Professor, Arthur and Dr Seward. The Professor told them about Lucy.

"Jonathan," said the Professor. "I believe the boxes you saw in Dracula's castle were the same as those found in the wrecked ship at Whitby."

"If they belonged to the Count, they would have been sent on to Carfax House," said Jonathan.

"So the Count is at Carfax," said Dr Seward. "At last I understand why my strange patient Renfield licked up my blood. Now I know who his master is. The Count has him in his power."

Later that night, Mina wrote in her diary.

After dinner, we discussed what to do next.

"I will tell you about Dracula," said the Professor. "He is neither alive nor dead. He is un-dead. He lives off the blood of the living. He can become invisible. He has no reflection. If we beat him, he is gone for ever. If he beats us, we become vampires like him. Do you wish to carry on?"

Of course, we all did.

"Very well," he said. "Dracula can be destroyed. He has no power in the daytime. He usually sleeps in his coffin. If his coffin is nearby he can move in the day but cannot do harm. He is afraid of garlic and the cross. We can kill him in his coffin. Without his coffin, he has nowhere to hide. He will have lots of coffins. We must find them all and make sure he cannot use them."

That night, the four men went to look for the coffins. They broke into the old chapel at Carfax House and found coffins stacked everywhere.

"Why does the Count need so many?" asked Jonathan.

The Count means to hide his coffins all over London. Then he will always be close to one. We must make sure he doesn't succeed!

The next day, Mina wrote in her diary again.

When the men had gone to the chapel, I went to bed. I lay awake. I felt tired, but I could not sleep. Something told me Dracula was near.

A white mist floated in front of my eyes. It poured like smoke through the window. Then it turned into a whirling pillar of cloud. Two red eyes fixed their gaze on me.

When I woke up late this morning, Jonathan had returned. I had slept for a long time, but I did not feel refreshed.

That night, the men returned to the chapel at Carfax. They placed a cross and a spray of garlic on every coffin.

"Dracula is out looking for new victims," said the Professor. "When he returns, he will find he can no longer use his coffins."

But Jonathan was worried.

A few hours later, Dr Seward went to check on Renfield, his patient. He found him in a pool of blood.

"It was the Master," Renfield whispered. "He was here. He said, 'I don't care about you any more. I've found a better victim who lives nearby.'

"I tried to fight him, but he threw me to the floor. Then he disappeared."

Renfield went limp. He was dead.

Dr Seward rushed to tell the Professor
what he had found.

"What can the Count mean by 'a better
victim who lives nearby'?" he asked.

"Mina!" answered the Professor.

The Professor and Dr Seward ran to Mina
and Jonathan's house. They burst in.
Jonathan woke up.

Standing over Mina was a dark, cloaked
figure.

The Professor grabbed a cross from his pocket and held it out. Dracula howled and let Mina go.

Then Dracula turned and crashed through the window. Dr Seward ran after him onto the balcony. Dracula had disappeared!

"We must find Dracula and destroy him!" said Jonathan. "We were too late to save Lucy, but Dracula will not take Mina."

"It will not be easy," said the Professor. "We scared him away but the Count has tasted Mina's blood. He has part of her now."

"Then we're beaten," Jonathan groaned.

"Not yet," said the Professor. "Dracula cannot use his coffins at Carfax House. There's only one place he can hide now."

CHAPTER 6

The final battle

"The Count will try to escape," the Professor said when they all met the next day.

"Where to?" asked Dr Seward.

"I don't know," said the Professor. "But perhaps we can find out.

"Mina, when the Count took some of your blood, he took part of you as well. Maybe that means you have become part of him. May I put you into a trance? We might be able to read his thoughts."

Soon Mina was in a deep trance.

"I hear water," she said. "Waves are beating against the sides of a ship."

"Dracula is sailing back to his castle," said the Professor.

"He has one coffin left and he is using it
to return home."

The Professor stood up. "We must follow him. We will travel by train. Dracula must not reach his castle!"

The next day, Mina, Jonathan, Arthur, Dr Seward and the Professor set off. They were determined to destroy Count Dracula.

After a long journey, they arrived at the port nearest to Dracula's castle.

When Dracula's ship didn't arrive, the Professor put Mina in another trance. They found out that Dracula had landed at a different port. He was already ahead of them on his way to the castle.

The local people told them that a band of gypsies had taken the Count's coffin. They were guarding him on his journey.

When the Professor and his friends heard this, they knew they had to overtake him. They travelled through deep forests. They took secret mountain passes that were too narrow for the cart carrying Dracula's coffin.

The air grew colder. Snow lay all around
them. But at last they overtook Dracula and
arrived before him at the castle.

It was an hour before sunset. Jonathan
remembered his last visit. He felt a thrill
of fear. Together, they all climbed up to the
castle gates.

Jonathan took them inside and down to the old chapel. There they found three coffins. The Professor opened the lids. In each coffin was a woman.

"These are the women who held me prisoner here," said Jonathan.

The Professor hammered a stake into the heart of each woman. Then he cut off their heads. As he did so, each one screamed. Then they crumbled into dust. They had disappeared for ever.

The Professor stood up, trembling. "They are at peace at last," he said.

The sound of horses came from outside. "Quick! The Count is here," said the Professor. "We are well armed. Get ready."

The sun began to sink behind the mountain tops. The gypsies appeared with a cart. They were armed with axes and knives. On the cart lay a long coffin.

The final battle started. The gypsies fought bravely. But the rifles of Jonathan, Arthur, Dr Seward and the Professor were too powerful for them. They fled, leaving the cart with Dracula's coffin.

As the sun was about to disappear, Arthur and Jonathan sprang onto the cart. They tore the lid from the coffin.

The Count lay inside. In a moment, when the sun had gone, he would rise up and kill. But that moment never came. Jonathan's knife tore into Dracula's throat just as Arthur's stake plunged deep into his heart.

Count Dracula's body crumbled into dust. The world was free of him for ever.

Dennis Hamley has written many novels and stories for children and young adults, including mysteries in the *Point Crime* series.

He is married, with a grown-up son and daughter and two cats. He does many school visits and writing workshops.

IMPACT
RETELLING
SET C